D0396090

THE ARRANGEMENT

Vol. 6

H.M. Ward

www.SexyAwesomeBooks.com
Laree Bailey Press

COPYRIGHT

This book is a work of fiction. Names, characters, places, and incidents are either the product of the author's imagination or are used fictitiously, and any resemblance to actual persons, living or dead, events, or locales is entirely coincidental.

THE ARRANGEMENT

Vol. 6

CHAPTER 1

Heart pounding, I press the button for the elevator a million times, but the doors don't open. My body is surging with too many emotions. It feels like I'm going to fall to pieces. I hear them behind me. Sean's voice rings out in my ears, but I don't want to listen. Nothing they say will fix this. I feel like there's an axe in my chest and I'm bleeding out. The sense of betrayal is strangling me and muddying my thoughts.

I don't wait. I run toward the end of the hallway and shove through the door. I'm in the stairwell. Before I know it, I'm running down the stairs as quickly as possible. Just as I fly down the first set of steps, the door bangs open. Sean is standing there, shirt open, and breathing hard.

I stop. Time freezes and I wish to God that we never met. His eyes lock with mine. His lips part like he's going to say something, but I don't want to hear it. I'm done. No, it's past that. I can't bear this. I can't take the lot I've been handed. It's strangling the life out of me. As it is, I can barely breathe. The moment shatters when I look away. I'm running, heart pounding, flying down the stairs. My hand grips the railing hard as my body whirls around when I reach the landing. My heels are slowing me down.

Sean's voice rings out behind me. "Avery, wait!" But I don't stop.

Footfalls follow close behind me growing louder and louder. There's no going back, not after this. Mind racing, I try to decide what to do, where to go. They both know the places I run to when I'm shaken, when life has brought me to my knees. My heel catches the edge of a step wrong and I stumble forward. My arms flail in front of me and I catch my balance.

"Damn it, Avery! Stop!" Sean is closer, so much closer. If he touches me, I'll scream. Emotions are building inside of me and the only thing that keeps me from shattering is that he isn't touching me. He can't touch me. I can't stop.

The balls of my feet smack each step, barely touching it as I fly down another flight. I'm huffing. Hysteria is closing in around me. I feel it slick over my skin like a snake. I can't choke it back down. I can't banish it. Sean calls out again, but I don't stop.

Just as I'm about to round another landing, there's a loud crash behind me. Sean stumbles forward after jumping from the stairs above. He curses as he lands and his knee buckles, knocking him toward me. The momentum sweeps us into the wall.

"You have the shittiest timing," he huffs. Sean's body is crushing me into the wall. He takes a deep breath and straightens, but leaves me trapped between his body and the wall. A hand rests on either side of my head. He leans into me. "It's not what it looks like."

I don't want to hear it. "I know what I saw."

I try to twist away from him. My heart is slamming into my ribs and my brain is telling me that it's going to break if I stay here. *He can't touch me. I have to leave. I have to.* Frantic, I try to twist away from him and duck under his arm, but Sean's hand juts out and grabs my wrist.

"Let me go," I growl. My voice is so low. I'm going to snap. I feel my mental rope—the one that holds me together—coming apart string by string.

Sean leans in close to my face. "No. You're wrong and if I let you go, I'll never see you again. Walk up the stairs, Avery."

I shake my head and try to pull away. "Go fuck the rest of my friends, and leave me alone."

"Avery." There's a warning tone in his voice, but I don't care.

I dig my nails into his arm and try to pry my wrist away. "I said leave me alone!" I scream the words in his face. They echo through the stairwell. The vibrations bounce back at us.

As I speak, I twist and fall to the floor. Sean can't hold me. My wrist comes free. I jump up and just as I start to run, he grabs me by the waist. I scream as I'm whirled around and hurled over his shoulder. My dress gets hiked up insanely high. Sean holds onto my legs at my thigh and tightens his grip. I kick and slam my fists into his back, but he doesn't let go. Sean turns and starts back up the stairs. The movement makes me stop flailing. I hold onto him, afraid of falling over the edge of the railing and down the center of the staircase.

He can tell I'm afraid. "You should have walked back up the stairs." That's all he says before his walk turns into a run. I bounce on his shoulder and cling to him like I'm going to die. A terrified scream rips from my throat. Sean finally hits the top landing and pushes back through the door. We're in the hallway and headed toward his room.

Mel's voice rings out as we approach. "Awh, shit. She's going to kill you when you put her down. You know that, right?"

Sean moves fast. He shoves past Mel and we're in his room. I hear the door close behind me. Mel leans against it and shakes her head before turning away. I want to scream at her, but just as I start to talk, I'm jostled. Sean's hands are around my waist. He lifts me from his shoulder, and tosses me on the bed. I yelp as I fall through the air and land on the mattress.

I dart upright, but before I can move Sean jumps on top of me, pinning me down. His face is too close to mine. His touch burns like acid. I writhe and try to break free, but I can't. I kick and scream. Sean watches me with those irritating blue eyes.

How could he be so cold? How the fuck could he do this to me, then drag me back here like it doesn't matter?

Sean's looking down at me. I can feel his eyes on the side of my face. "I'll let you go, but you have to look around first. Look at the room, Avery." Sean's voice softens.

He watches me, but I don't want to look. I stare at him defiantly. Anger is consuming me. Every muscle in my body is corded tight, ready to snap. My vision flickers at the edges and spots of red burst behind my eyes like fireworks. I'm so angry that I'm shaking.

My mind keeps replaying the past few weeks. They streak by like a movie that's playing too fast. I see Sean's face on the day I met him, that smile, then the kite hitting his head, and I remember the feeling of his lips on my body, and it's too much. I can't take it. Every thought, every memory is toxic. It's killing me. The urge to run shoots through me again. I lean forward like I'm going to say something and spit in his face.

Sean takes a deep breath and lets it out slowly. He wipes my saliva away with the back of his hand. "I deserved that, but not for this." His hands slip into my hair on either side of my face. He tilts my chin up and meets my gaze. "Please, look around." The way he says it is so frail, like he's given up.

It rips through me, but I can't calm down. When his hands fall away and he stands up, I jump off the bed and run straight at him like a crazy person. My fists bang into his chest and I'm screaming. Words fly out of my mouth and I don't even know what I'm saying. They tangle with tears and all logic is lost. I can't think. I wish to God that I couldn't feel. "I didn't want this! This wasn't supposed to be my fucking life! And you and your goddamn demons! I have my own! I can't live like this! I can't!

"I'm falling apart. It's killing me. I'm drowning and there's no way to stop it. When I fall asleep at night, I feel the water around my neck, cold like a metal noose. Every night the noose grows tighter and tighter. I wish I never met you! I'm not falling for your screwed-up shit anymore. I don't care how you feel. I don't care what I see!"

When I turn away from, Sean I'm shaking. There's a tremor that runs down my spine. It swallows me whole. My face is damp with cold sweat. I close my eyes hard and try to focus my blurring vision as I move across the room. I'm leaving. They can't stop me.

Sean says nothing. He watches me step toward the door without a word.

But Mel is there. She moves in front of the only way out, blocking it. She folds her arms over her chest and she shakes her head. "You are *not* leaving until you turn around."

"Get out of the way." My jaw locks and my eyes narrow. My fists tighten at my sides. Her eyes drop to my hands before returning to my face.

"Do you plan on punching the shit out of everyone who cares about you?"

"You don't care about me."

She throws her head back and laughs. "You're such a wreck that you can't tell your ass from your elbow right now. The man asked you to look at the room and you can't even do that. Your brain left your body the minute you stepped out of that elevator. Or was it earlier when you were fucking Henry Thomas? Maybe you left your brain with him?"

My jaw drops. It hangs open, but I don't breathe. I thought she was my friend. I thought Mel cared about me, but she doesn't. Betrayal winds its way up my throat and chokes me. I want to punch her. I want to scream at her, but I can't say anything. Then, when she brings up Henry, it's like a verbal bitch-slap.

"You were with Thomas?" Sean's voice is behind me.

I don't turn. I don't answer. I stare at Mel like she's a traitor.

Mel's tiger eyes bore into me. "You can think whatever the hell you want about me and you're right. I'm a slut. I'll do whatever I have to do to survive, but there is no way I'd betray you. Open your goddamn eyes, Avery, and look around.

"Look at me. Do I look like I've been working? Is my hair all messed up like yours? Am I covered in sweat? Is my dress wrinkled? Does the room like we had sex?"

I stare at her. My eyes flick over her dress and her hair. She looks pristine. It still doesn't mean anything. They could have showered. She could have hung her dress.

Mel unfolds her arms and steps toward me so we're nose to nose. She knows I don't believe her. "Turn around." She pushes my shoulder and I turn about half way. I can see the room out of the corner of my eye. My pulse is pounding in my ears like a distant drum.

Papers. There are papers everywhere. There's an open briefcase on the desk by the window. Pens and papers are all over the table. There's a pizza box with a few half-eaten slices on the floor in front of the television. The flat screen is flickering. An old movie is playing. The bed is made and the only place that's rumpled is where Sean put me a few minutes ago. My eyes sweep the room, taking it in.

"No," I say. "I know what I saw. I know what you do, what he wants. So, Sean was working before you came—"

Mel stands next to me and cuts me off. "Cut the crap, Avery. You know the truth. You see it. Nothing happened here. If it did, you know that man wouldn't be thinking a logical thought for the rest of the night. Besides, I still smell like a spring daisy." Mel lifts her arm and shoves her armpit in my face. "Sniff."

I swat at her and step away. "Stop it, Mel." I don't want to believe her, but I smell her deodorant and her perfume is still there. It's not mingled with sweat. She didn't shower. I finally see it, and the thought sinks in slowly.

Nothing happened here.

My mind knows, but my heart is stuck. I can't let it go. I don't know what to do. I stand there, staring. I don't look at Sean. I know what he looks like. I know how good he smells. His scent hit me hard in the stairwell. I know his after-sex scent and that's not it. My eyes move across the room, searching for any indication of sexual activity, but there isn't anything. It looks like Sean's been working and Mel's been eating.

Mel leans against the wall and folds her arms across her chest again. She glances at Sean and then back at me. "Avery?" I don't answer. "Say something."

I feel like I've been sucked into the center of a maze. I can't find my way out. Exhaustion, fear, and humiliation are all vying to dominate me. It's like having cymbals banging into the sides of my head over and over again. I'm ready to collapse. Every ounce of energy I had is gone.

Swallowing hard, I turn to her and pick at the only bone I can find. There's too much emotion and no release. I can't deflate. I need to fight. "You should have told me. Black gave you his information days ago. You should have said something to me!"

For the first time, Mel looks awkward. "I wanted to, but I didn't know what to do. I couldn't tell Black no and—"

My pointer finger is in her face. "You still should have told me. I can't take this, Mel. I can't. I don't know how you do it, but I can't." I shut my mouth and shake my head. I can't talk to her. I can't face Sean. It's too much.

"I have to go." My emotions are fried. I don't trust myself anymore, and I can't do this. I'm out the door before they can say another word, and this time no one follows me.

CHAPTER 2

It's so damn late, but I can't go home. I don't want to see Mel at the dorm, and I sure as hell can't tolerate Amber right now. Before I realize where I'm going, I'm wandering through Penn Station and boarding a train. Now, my head is tipped to the side against the window. There are a few other people scattered through the train car. For a long time, I just sit there and stare out the window, watching the world whip past in a blur of colored lights.

Numbness is consuming me. My phone is clutched in my hand. I flick it to life and dial. Marty answers, half asleep. "Vavery?" He yawns. I try to speak, but nothing comes out. I hear Marty sit up. "What's the matter?"

"Hey," I manage.

"Where are you?"

"On the train." My voice is too soft. It catches in my throat and I think about hanging up. The lights inside the train flicker and everything goes dark for a second before they blink back on. I stare at the houses crammed so close together, wondering about the people who live in them. I thought that would be my life. I thought I'd be in one of those houses one day. Things weren't supposed to go this way. My throat is so tight, so dry.

Marty is quiet for a second. He must stand, because I hear his mattress creak. "Taking a joyride?"

"Something like that."

The speaker crackles to life and announces the next stop. Marty must hear it because he says, "You're at Babylon, babe. You passed your stop."

"I'm not going home."

"Then, where are you going?"

I take too long to reply. I breathe, "I don't know."

The train slows as it approaches the platform. Marty's talking again. "Avery, get off the train and I'll come get you, okay?"

I don't answer. I look out the window at the parking lot. Unbidden memories flash behind my eyes like they're happening now. I see my parents park their car and take my small hands, as we walk toward the station. I'm four years old and smiling. They tell me about the play we're going to see in the city, and that there will be music and dancing. I can't stop smiling. They swing me between them. I laugh as my little feet kick in the air. Marty speaks and the memory shatters—he doesn't know what this place does to me.

"Avery? Did the train stop?"

"Yes."

"Get off. Go downstairs and wait for me. I'm already in my car. Did you get off the train?"

The night air chills my skin and I realize I've already exited the train. If I didn't call Marty, I might have passed this place without getting off. The platform is high, it's taller than the trees. I can see the school below and a parking lot that's mostly empty. The wind whips past me, tugging my hair as it blows. My red dress does little to keep me warm.

"I'm outside. I'm fine Marty. I'm sorry I called you." I'm staring like I'm lost in a dream.

More memories surface: Argyle Lake and winters with silver skates. Recollections of my Dad jumping up and down on the ice, telling me to come out, that it's safe. I was so afraid back then, but my parents made me feel safe. They chased away the monsters.

I wrap my arms around my middle. A guy walks past me and gives me a once over as he heads toward the staircase. My make-up is probably smeared all over my face.

I hear Marty's car start and realize he's talking to me. "...can call me anytime. I'll be there as fast as I can." I nod and hit END CALL.

My red dress draws attention, but the expression on my face keeps people away. I walk down the stairs and fold my arms over my chest. I try to wait for Marty, and pace inside the lobby of the station. I look at the benches, at the seats, and more memories pound into me. I can't stand it. It's like opening Pandora's box. There's no way to let one recollection slip past without summoning ten more. This place brings them back. And, it's not just the pictures and faces—I feel the hugs and distant laugher caress me lightly. It's as if I've been touched by a ghost.

That's it. I can't wait. I can't stay here. I turn quickly and push out the front door. I head down the sidewalk and I don't think about where I'm going. I don't think about anything. I'm not sure how much time passes when my phone rings again. I look at the screen and see a picture of Marty's smiling face with his 80's flipped collar and spike hair.

"Hey," I say after answering.

"Where are you? I'm in the station, but you're not here." Worry laces through his words.

I feel bad for making him worry. "I'm sorry, but I couldn't stay there. I'm walking on Locust." I'm not far from the station.

The truth is, once I left the building, there was only one place to go.

"I'll be right there." Marty hangs up.

I keep my phone in my hand and look at the houses. I stop in front of one and stare. A single sidewalk leads to the front door of a little Cape Cod style house. It's still the same pale yellow color as it was when we lived there. The tree in the side yard still has my tire swing from when I was a kid. It moves in the breeze, gently swinging. I glance at my old window, and then to my parent's window.

My gut twists, tying itself in knots too tight to bear. I clutch my stomach and sit down hard on the curb. I press my fingers to my temples and lower my head to my knees.

Breathe, Avery. Just breathe. It's my mother's voice. I hear it in my mind like she's really here, but I know she's not. I realize I can no longer remember the exact sound of her voice. It's a shadow now, missing the inflections that she had. A sob creeps up my throat and strangles me. I sit there like that for too long, lost in the past.

Headlights finally illuminate the street in two wide beams. I don't look up. Marty steps out of his car and hurries toward me. "Are you all right?"

I shake my head. I can't look at him. I can't tell him what I did with Henry. I hate myself. I hate what I've become. I don't want to relive anything about tonight. I don't want to tell him about Mel and Sean. Just thinking about it makes the panic return.

Marty holds out his hands. I take them and he pulls me up. I fall into his chest and he folds his arms around me. He kisses my forehead and says, "Bad night?"

"I don't want to talk about it."

"Then, don't. Come on. Let's get out of here before we get shot."

CHAPTER 3

The next morning I rub my eyes and roll over. My head is pounding. The bed beneath me creaks and I realize where I am. I feel the supple sheets and Marty's scent fills my head. I push up on my elbows and look around the room. Last night is a blur of tears and regret. Going to Babylon was a mistake. I figured I already had my heart ripped out of my chest. I didn't think I could make it worse. I was wrong.

"Hey lazy bones." Marty is wearing a pair of lacrosse shorts and no shirt. His hair is rumpled, but other than that he looks normal. There's no trace of a late night under his eyes.

"Hey." I look down at my clothes. I'm wearing one of Marty's old tee shirts. My red dress isn't in sight. Neither is my bra. I threw them on the floor last night and collapsed on the bed. "I feel like I was comatose. God…" I rub my head. It's still throbbing.

"Hang over?" Marty is sitting at the kitchen counter across from me. He has an efficiency apartment, which means his bedroom is in his living room. I can see the entire apartment. I haven't been over here much. It's decorated nicely, but not as nicely as he decorated my dorm room. I shove the thought aside even though something seems out of place.

"I wish. I could deal with that."

"Gonna tell me what happened?"

I stare at him. I feel like someone chopped me up and put me back together. It seems like every stich and every scar is showing. I wonder if I have bolts in my neck. I'm turning into a monster. I know it. I feel it. The pieces of me that remain are so small. "I caught Mel with Sean." His jaw drops. "Yeah, that's what I thought, but they said nothing happened."

"I'll bitchslap Mel for you."

"I already did."

Marty looks impressed. "No way. And you lived to tell about it. She's knifed people for doing less, you know."

"I know." I twist the sheet between my fingers as we talk.

"So, let's pretend that I ate too much glue when I was little, and that I don't fully grasp the implications of what you're saying. So what? I mean, you're still hooking, so who cares if another girl fucks your guy? I mean, you're doing it. Doesn't it seem a little bit hypocritical to be mad if Mr. Twisted decides to have sex with someone else?"

"Yeah, I'm a hypocrite. That's what had me in that funk last night." I say sarcastically and sigh as I rub my face with the heels of my hands.

"Then, spell it out."

I glance up at him. "It was who Sean was with that was the problem. Mel didn't tell me. She can't tell Black no, but she could have mentioned it to me."

"And what would you've done?"

I stare at him. "I don't know."

"He's not yours, Avery. And Mel's gotta work."

"You're taking her side?" I shoot daggers at him.

Marty waives his hands frantically, "No, but what do you want to happen here? Mel's your best friend. And you still have a thing for Sean. There's no happy ending with him, Avery."

I close my eyes and groan. "I don't want to talk about it."

"You need to. Deal with it. You got a shitty hand. Deal with it." I look up and Marty's eyes lock with mine. "Chose someone who can help you deal with it. Sean can't. He hasn't even faced his own shit, so he can't help you with yours."

My stomach dips. The way he's looking at me, the barely contained emotion in his eyes makes me look away. My heart thumps to life inside of me and I don't know why.

"How do you know he can't help me? Maybe Sean's has dealt with his past and—"

Marty laughs and folds his arms over his bare chest. "He's dealt with his ghosts as much as you have."

I bristle. "I've dealt with mine."

"No you haven't. That's why you're a mess. That's why you can't move forward. Stop making excuses. Stop feeling sorry for yourself. It won't change anything.

"Keep your close friends close, and walk through the fire already. There's a life waiting for you on the other side. I swear to God it gets better, but you'll never get there with a guy like that. Sean's pulling you down with him." Marty's gaze bores into me. His words are like stones falling from the sky. Each one hits me hard.

I feel naked, like he sees through me. I hate it. I want to pull the blankets up to my neck, but I know it won't hide anything. He knows me too well. "You think he's a crash and burn?"

Marty gives me a look. "I think he's poison. I think he burnt up a long time ago. I think everything he touches turns to ash. I don't want him to touch you anymore. I can't stand to see you like this. You were doing well before he came along." Marty takes a sip of his coffee.

"Is that why you chased him off at the hospital?"

One of Marty's brows lifts and he gives me a lopsided grin. "You knew about that?"

I nod. "Yeah, I did. I didn't understand why you did it." I'm looking at the sheets that I'm twisting in my grip when I feel the bed next to me dip. The springs make a metallic sound and I hear Marty inhale. He runs his fingers through his hair.

"I chased him off because I can't let you do it." Marty is sitting next to me. I turn toward him and keep my eyes on his chest, on the smooth toned skin. I'm afraid to look up. This feels weird. It feels like he's being possessive, but not in a brotherly way. The way he's looking at me is so adoring, so perfect. *He's gay. There's no way in hell he feels anything toward me, not like that.* I think I've gone crazy until I feel his hand on my knee. His touch makes me so nervous. I don't know where the feelings are coming from.

I glance up at him. "Do what?" Our eyes lock and something inside of my chest tightens. My stomach flips and nervous energy shoots through my veins. This is impossible. The only pull I should feel toward Marty is friendship. I swallow the lump in my throat.

"I can't let you lose sight of who you really are—that red dress and those clothes—that's not you. You're not a call girl. You're Avery Stanz. You're a brilliant, caring, young, beautiful woman who has so much potential, so much life left in her. She's capable of wonderful things. She's the best person I know. You can't give up on her, because I haven't. She'll pull through. She's still in here," he gently presses a finger to my heart. He says everything I ever needed to hear, but no one ever said.

I bite my lower lip to keep it from trembling. The emotions that I buried in the back of my mind start to leak out. "Marty…"

His hand returns to his lap. "Don't tell me she's gone, because she's not. Don't tell me you can't go backwards, that you can't be who you were. You haven't changed, Avery. You're still you."

I swallow hard and feel my chest cave in. Why does he do this to me? Every time I pick myself up and rebuild the walls, Marty tears them down. I need them to survive. I can't stand on my own anymore. No matter what he says, I know I'm too weak.

"Sentimentality won't change anything, Marty. After everything I've done, after everything I did to get here—" I suck in air and shake my head. When I glance up into his eyes, I see my reflection. It looks the same. It looks like the Avery from before my life spun out of control, but she's not. That girl is gone.

Marty takes my hands and squeezes them hard. "Then don't waste it. You made huge sacrifices to get where you are, but that's all they were. Those choices don't own you. You own them.

"Come on, who said, *regret is for pussies?* Who said that you only get one life, live it the best you can and don't look back? You did. And out of everyone I ever met, you're the only one who has the right to say it. You lived through hell, and you pulled yourself out. Don't attach yourself to someone who's going to drag you back there."

I'm looking at my hands while he speaks. This conversation feels too personal, but I need to hear it. There's no one to tell me to suck it up, to get up and keep going. The girl who felt that way about regret gives me a mental high-five. She's still in there, fighting to break free.

I lift my gaze and look at Marty. "Why do you put up with me?" I smile sadly at him and shake my head.

"Because…" Marty smiles at me, like the answer is so plainly obvious. "I love you."

CHAPTER 4

He's said those words before, but they never sunk in the way they do now. I smile at him—like I don't understand, like I know he's gay and doesn't mean it that way. Marty watches my face, looking for a reaction, but I don't want to react. I don't want anything to change. Maybe I'm making a big deal out of nothing. My emotions are a jumble. I don't trust my senses. It's just not possible, so I disregard the weird tension between us.

Mentally, I laugh for being so stupid. He doesn't *love me*, love me.

I smile at him and say it back. "I love you, too."

Marty doesn't move. He sits on the edge of his bed and watches me. The look makes my stomach dip. God, I'm messed up. I'm not even feeling things right anymore. He's gay. That isn't what he meant. He doesn't like me like that, but even as I think the thoughts, I notice his eyes dip to my lips. The sound of my breath fills my head, and my pulse pounds harder. Marty leans in ever so slowly. He pauses right before his mouth touches mine. We're a breath apart. I'm frozen. Half of me thinks that this isn't happening, that I'm wrong about him. I don't know what to do.

Marty's breath is warm. I feel it pass across my lips as he exhales slowly. Just as he lowers his lashes, a loud thud comes from the door. It's directly across from us. We both turn our heads just in time to see Mel walk inside.

When Mel looks up, she laughs like something is horribly funny. "Talk about things that look wrong."

Marty jumps up and grabs his drink from the counter. "Why did I agree to be key buddies with you?" He glances at me and holds my gaze for a moment before turning away. I have no idea what's going through his head.

Mel plants her hands on her hips. "I don't know. That was kind of crazy once you start thinking about it."

"You're not supposed to let yourself in whenever you want," Marty grumbles.

I glance at Mel and then Marty. When did they exchange keys? They must be hanging out without me.

Mel claps her hands together. "Well, let's get going, ladies. It's already late and I want my pancakes." I look at her for a second and feel really uncomfortable. My gaze drops. She notices. "Awh no. Mel does not do awkward, so cut that shit out. Last night never happened. You understand?"

"We need to talk."

"Hell no, we don't need to talk about a damn thing." She won't look at me now.

I scoot to the edge of the bed and throw my feet over the edge. They land on the floor. I press my fingers to my temples and try to navigate this mess as best I can. To do that, I need details. I want to know what occurred between them, if anything. The whole situation is too weird, especially with Marty watching me. I glance at him for half a second. He's sipping his coffee, avoiding my gaze. Was he seriously going to kiss me? I feel like I'm losing my mind.

"What happened?" I ask Mel bluntly. Blunt works best with her. "I need to know. When you showed up last night and Sean opened the door, what'd he do? Did you guys do anything?" My voice catches on the last word. The thought makes my stomach sour. What if they kissed? What if they…did what me and Henry did. I don't think I could bear it, but I ask. I have to know.

Mel works her jaw and stares at Marty with eyes that are too big for her head. Marty remains perched on his stool and doesn't look back. "Is she deaf? She didn't just ask me that, did she?"

Marty turns. His brows flick and he glances at me out of the corner of his eye before grabbing a towel from the closet. "She did and she's on the edge, Mel. Push her off and I'll bust your ass."

Mel's head jerks as her jaw drops open. "Are you threatening me, Princess?"

"Damn right, I am." Marty's voice is too deep, too stern. His gaze narrows as he stares Mel down. "She's been through enough shit to last a lifetime. Ask her where I picked her up last night. That'll tell you everything." Marty looks over at me like he wants to say something, but he doesn't. Instead he disappears into the bathroom and the shower turns on. My gaze follows after him. How did he know? I never told him where I grew up, but he seems to realize the devastation that brought me to my knees last night. Going to the old house didn't help.

Mel takes Marty's seat at the counter. She looks at me. I'm sitting on the edge of the bed. "Where'd you go last night?"

I shrug. "It doesn't matter."

She jabs her thumb toward the bathroom and says, "He thinks it does. Where were you?"

I look up. Mel is severe, but there's worry in her eyes. "What'd you do with Sean?"

She stiffens. We stare each other down for a moment. Mel finally rolls her eyes and the tension in her back gives way. "Fine. I'll go first. When I showed up at his door, he asked if you were okay. He didn't put it together until I told him that Black sent me, that I was there because he ordered a call girl. He stared at me and asked me in. I can't tell him no, and I didn't think he'd do anything. He's too wrapped up in you." She shakes her head and looks up, smiling at me. "First thing he says is, 'what do you want to eat?' He orders me a pizza and goes back to work. I watched a couple of movies while he pulled his hair out trying to get some techno-nerd thing to work out on paper. The arrangement was that he'd tell Black that I was phenomenal and I wasn't supposed to tell you anything. But you got there early and the shit hit the fan."

"He didn't kiss you?"

She smirks. "He didn't touch me. Not even a handshake." My gaze falls to the floor. I don't know what to think. Mel's voice snaps me back to reality. "Now you, where'd you go last night?"

I shove my hands into my hair and rub my scalp with my fingertips. When I look up at her, I say it. I just spit it out because Marty tattled. "Home. I went by the house, okay."

Mel's larger than life expression falters. It's gone in a flash. She's off the stool and next to me, but I don't want her pity. I can't stand it when people act like I'm falling apart. It's already happened. I wish they'd just accept me the way I am, because I'm all fucked up and no amount of sympathy is going to change that.

"And..."

I'm off the bed, standing, pacing. I move too much when I'm stressed and I have more anxiety than I can manage. "And nothing. Marty picked me up out front." I don't tell her the memories that flooded my mind. I don't tell her about the train station or the walk down those streets. There are no words. Mel cut her family off. Mine was ripped away from me.

The bathroom door opens and Marty walks out. He's wearing dark jeans with a ripped knee and a form fitting tee shirt the same color as his eyes. His golden hair is tousled, like he just rubbed it with a towel. I stare at him. I wonder if he slept next to me, but I'm afraid to ask, afraid of what's happening to us.

Mel glares at him. "You knew about this—you knew she went to her old house and didn't call me?" she snaps at Marty.

Marty is looking at me with those big brown eyes. There's an unreadable expression on his face. It's like he just figured out how incredibly messed up I am. "I didn't realize it was her childhood home."

She pinches the bridge of her nose and sighs. Mel ignores Marty and turns back to me. "So, what are you going to do now? You can't handle this guy, Avery."

"I can't handle this life, Mel. I'm up to my neck in bills." I round on her. I'm sick of people thinking they know what it's like to be in my shoes. They don't. Even Mel has no idea. The muscles in my neck are so tense that my voice sounds strangled. "Do you know what I dream about? Do you know what I see when I close my eyes at night? Water. It's everywhere and I can't swim anymore. It's exhausting. I stop swimming as the sea creeps up my shoulders, and then my neck until the top of my head goes under. Every fucking night, it's the same dream. I drown in black water."

Mel is quiet for a moment. "Did going home help? Did you have the dream last night?"

I think about it. I'm not sure. "I didn't dream anything last night."

I wonder why. I always have nightmares. Some are worse than others, but it's a normal part of my life. They started when my parents died and never went away. There are two dreams. In one I'm alone and drowning in an unending ocean. In the other, I'm screaming, telling my parents not to go, but they can't hear me. It rips my heart out of my chest every time, making all the scars ache like the accident just happened.

I feel Marty's gaze on the side of my face. I turn and look at him. "What?" I wish he'd say whatever it is that he's been thinking. I'm too brain dead to figure it out.

He smiles at me and looks away. "Nothing."

Mel watches the two of us. Her gaze flicks between me and Marty, like she's trying to figure out a puzzle. She shakes her head and says, "Come on. It's pancake time. Get this girl some clothes and let's get going." Mel claps her hands together and rubs. Marty grabs a pair of sweat pants from his closet and tosses them to me.

I decide to eat first and shower later. Maybe some fresh air and food will clear my head.

CHAPTER 5

I manage to go to a few of my classes, but I'm so tired. When I walk back to the dorm, I'm thinking about Sean. I wish he was here. I wish my life made sense. Nothing is stable. It feels like everything is shifting beneath my feet. Every time I think I figured things out, the world gets tipped on its side again. I can't stand it. I'm clinging, hanging on but it doesn't make a difference. It doesn't matter how much I try, nothing changes for the better.

As I walk through the parking lot, I glance over at my car. Sean is sitting on the hood. His jacket is zipped up to his neck. It's freezing outside. He slips off the hood and rushes over. I stop and stare at him, like he's an apparition.

"Hey."

"Hey," I say back, still shocked to see him. My mood is so fragile. I know what I need to say, I just don't want to. "Sean, this isn't working out—"

"I know. I just wanted to check on you. Last night was…" he lets out a jagged breath and runs his hands through his hair.

"Intense." The wind blows hard. I fold my arms around my middle and shiver. I still don't have a winter coat. "There's no way we can do this, Sean. I'm not allowed to have relationships and I don't think you really want one. If you did, you wouldn't be calling Black."

Sean presses his lips together and looks away. A dusting of dark stubble lines his rosy cheeks. "You're right. So what now?" He looks up at me from under his lashes. He's so beautiful and so completely messed up.

I stand there, my mouth hanging open for a moment, just staring at him and basking in the absurdity of the situation. I'm the hooker he can't get over. He's beautiful and I'm a train wreck. We're both beyond repair. Maybe there's no hope for either of us.

Sean watches me too closely for someone who doesn't care. His sapphire eyes finally flick up to my face. "Do you want me around? I think that's the question at the most basic level. I'm not worth keeping. I know that, but I need to hear it from you."

"Don't do self-deprecation, Sean." I look away. There are students walking across the parking lot. Marty and Mel will flip out if they see him here. "Where's your car?"

Sean jabs his thumb behind him. "I'm on the chrome monster you liked."

"Let me grab my jacket and helmet so we can go somewhere and talk." I go to turn away, and then look back at him and add, "If you think it's worth the bother."

"You are definitely worth the bother. I'll wait for you." Sean looks at me in a way that makes my stomach dip. It feels ominous, like he's really saying that he'll wait for me, forever.

I return to the parking lot a few moments later, wearing the gear he gave me with a clingy black sweater. As I zip the jacket, I feel Sean's eyes slip over me. "Ready." I throw my leg over the back of the bike and we're off.

Sean jumps on the Parkway and when we stop, we're at Sunken Meadow. It's a state park on the north shore. The beach is rocky, but there's a boardwalk and a little place to grab a snack. Sean fastens our helmets to the bike. We go to the little snack shop and order coffee. Sean hands me my steaming cup.

We go back outside and stroll down the boardwalk. It's fairly empty, because it's too cold for sane people to be strolling along the beach. The air smells like it's going to snow. It has the sharp crisp scent. I breathe it in deeply.

I finally say, "I have no idea where to start, so I'll just jump in. The hookers bother me. I don't understand why you still need that."

Sean nods and looks straight ahead. The wind ruffles his hair, tossing it every which way. "That's a good place to start. I don't like you sleeping with other guys, but it's something you have to do. It's how I ended up with you. I wish you'd stop, but I can't ask you that. I know what it means if you do. I know what you'd be giving up." Sean glances over at me. "I don't..." He presses his lips together and starts over. "I need them, the nameless faces, because it's the only way I can deal with the pain. When it's too much, I call. I take control back—"

"By having sex with strangers—"

"By dominating another person. By controlling them so thoroughly that I'm distracted from my life. Fear makes sense to me. They should be afraid of me." Sean's eyes glaze over as he speaks. He's breathing hard, like memories he wants to forget are pounding into him.

I stop walking. Sean slows and looks back at me. "That's why you can't do it with me? Because..." I'm not a stranger, because he knows me.

"You're not afraid of me. I know you and I want to make you happy, not scared."

Sean tucks a strand of hair behind my ear. I'm lost in his gaze, in his voice. I hate this. I wish he'd take me in his arms and let the past go. I don't realize it until the thought fully forms in my mind.

I laugh. "I'm a hypocrite. I was with someone last night and you didn't even ask me about it." I groan and rub my face with the heel of my hand.

"You're not wrong to ask about my, uh, preferences. It says something about me. And I'd like to know what you did, and who you did, but I don't think I could bear hearing the details. I don't want to share you and the thought that Thomas has had you twice—" Sean's fists clench at his sides and he lets out a rush of air. "I can't even think about it."

I smile at him. I didn't notice before, but I see it now. "You're jealous?"

"Jealous is an understatement. I want you for myself, but I don't want to hurt you. You're already hurting so much. You've become an enigma, and I don't know what to do about it."

We walk over to the railing and look out at the waves. "Then, maybe we shouldn't do anything."

Sean is leaning forward on the rail, but when I speak he straightens and turns toward me. "You want to go our separate ways?"

"Maybe," I say weakly. "We survived apart for a long time. Ever since we met, it feels like everything is spinning out of control." I laugh bitterly. "I can't tell you how many times I thought about trying to be what you need, about letting you do whatever you wanted to do to me." I stare at my fingernails like they're fascinating.

Sean is still. He's barely breathing. "You have?"

I nod, then smile like it's a stupid idea. "We can't go there, can we? I mean, that place isn't for us. And it doesn't matter what I offer you, you'll still need that control. I don't see how it would work anyway. Even if I let you do it once or twice and we have sex that way, that's all you have with me, once or twice. After that, I won't be as freaked out. I'll know what you're going to do and you won't get your, uh, reprieve." When I finish talking, I look up at him.

Sean's lips are parted. He looks so torn. I think he's going to say something, but he turns back to the railing and leans on it. Sean squeezes his hands together, wringing them tightly. "I can't believe you thought about doing that for me."

"I would have, I just don't see the point. It won't last, and then what? Then, we're back here asking the same questions with the same problems. I'll still be a call girl and you'll still be ordering my friends to give you what I can't. It sucks." I swallow the rest of my coffee and toss the cup in a wastebasket that's on the other side of Sean.

When I reach past him, my arm brushes his and he jumps. Sean steadies himself and closes his eyes for a second. "It sounds like you've already made up your mind."

"Part of it, yeah. I shouldn't see you anymore."

"But…?"

"But I can't stay away from you. I know what you're talking about with the pain becoming unbearable. The only thing that breaks it for me is you. Something about you makes me feel like I might pull through even though, I'm inches away from a crash. It's stupid, but—"

He puts his hand over mine. "It's not stupid. I know exactly what you mean."

Looking into his eyes, I ask, "So what now? I'm not okay with you doing other girls."

Sean tosses his coffee into the trash can. Then he puts his hands around my waist and tugs me to him. Our hips line up and press into each other. He tilts his head to the side. "I'm not okay with you being with other guys. How far did you go the other night? Can you tell me? Will you tell me?"

I smile softly. This is my Sean. This is the one I want, the imperfectly perfect version that's vulnerable. "Will I tell you? Do you really want me to?"

He nods. His eyes are locked on mine. Sean swallows hard, watching me, waiting for an answer that he doesn't want to hear. He leans in and presses his forehead to mine. "Please, Avery, tell me. Not knowing is worse than knowing."

I take a deep breath and put my hand on his shoulder. "Are you sure you want to know?"

Sean looks up from under his lashes. He presses his lips to mine for a second and nods. "Yes."

This is the weirdest conversation I've ever had. It's like he's asking me to hurt him, but some of his assumptions are wrong. I lower my gaze. My voice is soft. "We kissed, he touched me—ran his hands over my body—and saw me in the outfit you picked out." Sean is so tense, but he doesn't speak. He continues to look at me like I'm slipping away from him. "Should I go on?"

"Yes." His jaw locks after he says the word.

"He kissed my neck and my breasts before he…" I'm breathing too hard. I can't tell him this stuff. It looks like it's killing him. The pain on his face makes me cut to the last part. "Sean, he hasn't had me yet."

He blinks like he couldn't have possibly heard me right. "What?"

"Henry likes me. He wanted to ask me out, but since I'm working for Black—"

"He can't."

"Right, so he ordered me. I didn't have sex with him, yet."

"Yet?"

I nod. "He wants me again. I'll end up having sex with him this weekend. It's what he wants."

Sean holds me closer. "What do you want?"

"It doesn't matter what I want, I don't—"

"Tell me. Do you want him? Would you choose to be with him? He's a good man. He's everything I'm not. He'd be good to you, Avery."

I smile at him. "I don't want Henry. I want you. The thing is, I can't get all of you. There's a piece you won't give, something you won't share. Without that, I don't see how we can be anything to each other." I thread my fingers through the hair at the nape of his neck and twirl a lock of his hair.

Sean smiles, but it's brief. He closes his eyes and just breathes for a moment. "You're the only other girl at Black's that will do anything?"

"Yes, but—"

"Then I'm ordering you this weekend. We can try it, maybe."

"Are you sure you're not just trying to keep me away from Henry?"

He grins. "That's an added bonus."

CHAPTER 6

The next morning I'm sitting in the center of the classroom in Psych. I'm in a chair and another student, one I don't really know, is sitting across from me with a pen and paper in her lap. Our instructions are to practice the practical application of the techniques we learned during the semester.

I slouch back in my chair. Butterflies swirl in my stomach. I hate being in front of everyone. The other fifty or so students lean forward and get ready to watch. We'll be practicing basic counseling responses for the next three days. Case one, Avery Stanz. Good thing no one knows how screwed up I really am. I'm wondering if this girl will be able to pull down my walls and get at what makes me tick. I doubt it. I fold my arms across my chest. I'm the poster child for uncooperative participant.

The professor, Dr. Pratz, is standing in front of us. He's a tall slender man who's nearly bald save some white hair around his temples. He's wearing a Polo shirt and a pair of kakis. The soles of his shoes are worn through and the man is wearing different colored socks. Sometimes I wonder if he does stuff like that to see if we notice, because those of us going into this field need to notice and figure out what it means.

Dr. Pratz is addressing the class, explaining the order of the practicum. "Avery and Emma will have five minutes to talk. Emma's job is to guide the conversation to help Avery recognize her feelings on whatever subjects come up. During this exercise if either of you uncover a landmine, then the conversation will end. The purpose of this assignment is to help your client identify their emotions. That's it." He turns to us. "You have five minutes. Go!" He presses a button on the side of his watch and sits down on an empty seat in the front row.

Emma is nervous. She has light brown hair that she tucked behind her ears. She has on jeans and a pink sweater with pearl earrings. I don't think we'd get along by the looks of her. Emma looks like someone who has an easy life. I can see it in her eyes.

Emma's sitting at the edge of her chair. She shifts in the seat and looks up at me, flashing an anxious smile. "So, Avery, tell me how you're doing today."

"I'm fine."

"Avery," Dr. Pratz interrupts, scolding me, "you need to be at least semi-cooperative for this assignment, Miss Stanz. A real patient would be more cooperative."

"Not a teenager," I counter.

"You're not a teenager. Speak in full sentences please. And yes, I will interrupt if either of you needs it." He presses the button on his watch again. "Resume."

I straighten in my chair a little. "I'm doing okay today."

Emma looks at Dr. Pratz, but he doesn't interject again. "It sounds like you're a little tense. Is something bothering you?"

I shake my head and pick at my fingernails. "Nothing really. Just the normal end of semester stress and trying to juggle my time."

"Oh, do you usually have trouble with that?"

"No." I don't want to talk in front of all these people, but I'm being graded. I add, "It's just lately my time seems to get away from me. Add that to the end of semester assignments and I'm swamped. It's nothing major. Summer will come and then I'll have too much time. Time's like that, right? We either have too much or too little. It's never spot-on." I smile at her.

Emma nods. "What are the major things that consume your time?"

"Work and school."

"I understand that can be difficult. Where do you work?"

Crap. I straighten a little bit more and lie. "At a steakhouse."

"Stop," Dr. Pratz interrupts and steps between us. He turns to Emma. "Do you feel like you're making progress?"

Emma squirms in her seat. "Yes, I think so."

"Avery, since we only have a few minutes here, throw her a bone. Resume." He steps back and the clock is ticking again.

Throw her a bone? How the hell do I do that? I try to think of something that she can run with that won't make everyone get a glimpse into my mind. I chose something that seems harmless. "My friends are stressing me out. One is really stressing me out. He keeps saying he'll change, but he doesn't." How's that for a bone? I won't say it's Sean, but that should give her enough to work with for a few moments.

Dr. Pratz nods at me, pleased. Good.

Emma presses her lips together. Her forehead is creased with worry. "Ah, so it sounds like you don't think that people can change?"

"People don't change."

"So you completely disregard change theory? You don't believe a person can change when they set their mind to it?"

"No, and change theory is just that—a theory. People don't change. Name one person who truly changed." Emma opens her mouth, but says nothing. I prod her. "Come on. Anyone."

"Stop." Dr. Pratz says. He stands and steps between us. He says to Emma, "She commandeered the conversation. It's your job to control it. Steer it back so that the questions follow the path you want to take or God knows where you'll end up. Resume."

Emma swallows hard. "Why does this friend need to change?"

Because he's twisted and wants to make me cower in fear before he has sex with me. "To get over his past."

"Did something traumatic happen to him?" I nod. "I understand. So tell me, how do you think a person gets over something traumatic from their past?" I falter. The smug look on my face drops. She sees it and dives in. "Did something happen to you? Do you feel like you can't change? Do you feel trapped?"

My heart is pounding and a cold sweat breaks out on my forehead. I try not to show it, but it's like everyone can sense she found something. I stare at her like I want to pound her head in when we're in the parking lot later. I try to keep my voice light and my face expressionless, but it's impossible. I'm too bitter, too resentful because of what happened. "Yes."

"Did it change you?"

I nod. We learned that if a person decides that they want to change, that they can. Something has to change inside their mind before the change is complete. But that's not what happened to me. I didn't decide to become this way. I woke up one day and the change was forced on me. I glance at Dr. Pratz, hoping he'll stop her, but he doesn't. Emma asks, "Is that why you think people can't change, because you can't change back?"

Something twitches and it's like she touched a match to my mind. The entire class is utterly still, watching me. I stare at her. Changing by choice is not possible. If it was, I wouldn't be like this.

"People don't change." I manage. My throat is too tight, my voice is too strained.

"Do you want to change your life? Is it possible that you're the one who has the problems accepting change and not your friend?"

I stiffen. I forget that I'm in front of a classroom filled with people for a second. My emotions are too raw. "No, it's because some changes just don't happen. Some changes can't happen. Some people are too stuck, too broken. They can't be fixed, so it doesn't matter what you ask or how you frame it because the end result is always—"

Dr. Pratz cuts me off, "Time." I realize that Emma got to me. I'm not even sure how she did it, but she did. Allowing people to pick at mental sore spots is insane. None of those places have healed. I feel stupid.

Dr. Pratz continues, "Emma, very good, but you should never go through someone's mind randomly pressing buttons to see what happens. When you encounter a sore spot like the one you just found, it could be anything from a day-old ego bruise, to a decades-old abuse scar. If you press a button that's still raw, it turns into a landmine. You'll lose control of the session and your client.

"That's enough for today. Class dismissed." Dr. Pratz turns to Emma and me, "Please grab your things and follow me back to the counseling center."

Emma protests, "I have a class after this."

"Then go, I'll show you another time. Avery, come with me." Dr. Pratz is out the door before I have my books. I chase after him. He's so damn tall that it takes forever to catch up. When I fall in step with him, he looks over at me. "I can see it, you know."

I already know what he means. He knows I'm messed up. There's no guessing for guys like him. It's communicated without saying a word. "I know."

"Do you want help?"

I stare straight ahead and clutch my books to my chest. "No one can help me."

"Mmmm. A word of caution then— ghosts will haunt us unless we confront them. Until then, they have a way of invading every aspect of our lives and ripping it apart at the seams."

"Like a poltergeist."

"Exactly." We approach a door and he pulls it open, allowing me to walk inside first. It's the school's counseling center.

This is where I want to do my graduate work. If I continue to work for Black, I can start this summer. I'm excited and nervous to be here. I want to help people, but I need so much help myself. It really makes me wonder if I can do it. For a while, I thought all that pain would make me better at this job, but now I'm not so sure. Sometimes pain just hurts.

Dr. Pratz walks to the front desk, grabs his messages, and I follow him back to his office. "Sit."

I'm not sure what he wants, but I take a seat. "Avery, I know you want to be admitted to the grad school next year. It's a very rigorous program and I honestly have concerns about you being able to carry the course load."

This is news to me. Panic sparks to life in the pit of my stomach. "I can do it. I know I can. I maintained my GPA for undergrad. I had a bump, but I recovered."

He presses his palms together and looks at me for a moment. His dark eyes show nothing but concern, but it still makes my stomach dip. "You're right. Earlier this year, your grades were lacking. They improved, but I feel like you have some issues distracting you from your course work. Is it something you want to talk about?" I shake my head and give him an awkward smile. "If you ever want to talk, I'm here. I want to see you excel, Avery."

"I've found a way to begin grad school this summer. I can take a lighter course load, but attend year round, if you think that I should. Dr. Pratz, I really need this. I've worked so hard to get here. I promise that I'll give it my undivided attention."

"Avery, I like the idea of you spreading out your course load over the summer. Maybe that would allow you to lighten your work schedule. Your graduate scholarship is still being determined. The next few months are important. Attending this summer might be a very good option for you. One of the things you need to learn is to set reasonable expectations for yourself. If you constantly stretch yourself thinner and thinner, you'll snap."

"Yes sir."

We chat for a few more moments, and by the time I leave his office, I realize that my future plans may be beyond my reach. I need to ask Miss Black for fewer appointments and more money.

CHAPTER 7

The weather has turned frigid. Big thick flakes are falling from the sky as I trek across campus. When I finally get back to the room, Amber is cursing, getting ready for her night class. She tugs a sweater over her head and glares at me. "I hate the snow."

"Then move to Florida." Amber scowls and hurries out the door.

I sit on my bed for a moment. When I was younger snow made me so excited, so happy. As soon as there was enough snow covering the ground, I do the same thing every single time—built a snowman. I wonder if it's crazy, if I should do things like that anymore. I walk across the room to the window and look outside. It's still snowing. A smile slowly spreads across my face. Screw it. I don't care if people think I'm crazy. I'm going.

Taking my book bag, I dump out the contents on my bed before heading over to my dresser. I grab what I need and make my way down to my car. I still can't believe Sean repaired it for me. I grin at the old girl and pat the hood like she's a horse. "I would have missed you."

I slip inside and turn the key. The car starts right up. The interior is new and shiny even though it's decades old. I run my fingers along the dashboard, wondering if Sean changed anything else. It looks new. I slide the control across and turn on the heater. I keep my hand on the lever, expecting to get blasted with white smoke, but it never comes. He fixed the heater. I smile to myself. I'm not wearing a jacket. It's like Sean knew that and had the heater repaired. Normally, all the heat would have gone out the window, but it doesn't. My window is up. I lean forward and roll it down.

Ah! It moves! Oh my God! The window works! This is my car, but he brought it back to life. It doesn't stall anymore. I don't have to drive with two feet. It runs, like a real car. I sit there grinning as snowflakes cover the windshield. I'm almost afraid to try it, but I have to. I flick the wipers and they turn on. The wiper blades swoosh up and then down. Then they do it again.

"He fixed everything." I glance at the passenger seat and figure the seatbelt works too.

I take a deep breath. I can't stop smiling. I know exactly what I'm going to do. I pull out of the lot and head to the parkway. I drive east as the snow comes down harder and harder. By the time I get there, there's a blanket of white covering the ground. It's pristine and perfect.

I turn into the old cemetery. Snow lines the top of the headstones. I drive down the lane to my parents' plot and shut the engine.

I grab my bag and get out. There are a couple of inches of snow on the ground. It isn't much, but it's enough. I make a snowball and start rolling it around. It gets bigger and bigger before I roll it over to my parents' grave.

I talk to them as I do it. I tell them about everything that's going on, about how my life is getting away from me. I love a man who doesn't love me back. I'm a call girl. I finally manage to talk about that. "I don't like it. It's not what I thought it would be. I don't think I'm the kind of girl who sleeps around, so it feels really weird. Besides, I hate all the lying. It feels like I'm lying to everyone lately."

I roll around another snowball as I talk, then bring it over and stack it on the other one. I make a third snowball and roll it around, and then put it on top of the other two when it's the size of a pumpkin. My snowman is vertically challenged. I pack more snow on his belly and smooth it out. When I'm done, I stand in front of him. The snowman is a little shorter than me. I grab a scarf and the buttons from my bag. I press two hot pink sparkly buttons into his eyes and wrap a pink scarf around his neck. So he's a transvestite snowman. I like pink. I continue to talk to my parents as I finish decorating my snowman and the flow of words finally dries up.

When I'm done, I straighten, suck in the cold air, and look at their headstone. Memories flicker across my mind. My mom loved the first snowfall. My dad had told me the story of how they meet so many times that I'll never forget. They were both teenagers and had gone out sledding. Their sleds collided and it was fate. When I was a kid, they'd take me to Cardiac Hill at Sunken Meadow. They'd retell that same story every time. Winter was always filled with warm memories.

I smile to myself. I feel okay right now. I feel like I can bounce back and get on with things. I have to talk to Miss Black later. I wish to God my parents were still alive. I wish I didn't have to live this way, but wishing never made anything come true. It's time to stop feeling sorry for myself. I can do this. I have to. I will.

I glance up and look past the enormous tree. My gaze lands on Amanda Ferro's grave. There are footprints in front of it. Sean must have been here. I look around for him, but he's gone. Before I realize what I'm doing, I'm walking toward the grave. I stop in front of it and look down at the blanket of white. I don't know what comes over me, but I make a snowball in my hand. I roll it around and pack the snow together until there's a snowman next to her headstone.

Sean would have had a family. They would have gone Christmas shopping. His wife would have been making pot roast and wintery foods that fill the house with delicious scents. Instead, she's here with their only child, and Sean is alone.

I'm alone.

I turn away and walk back to my car. I drive off before Sean can materialize. I wonder how long he watched me or if he noticed me at all.

CHAPTER 8

I'm sitting in Miss Black's office. It's late. She's wearing a slim black suit that accentuates her thin frame. She looks regal. Miss Black has this air about her that's completely intimidating. The more I get to know her, the more I don't like her. The first day we met, she seemed nice, but I think that was a mask. The real Miss Black is a savvy business woman and often has a ruthless look in her eye—especially when it comes to me.

I'm dressed in old jeans with a torn knee and an oversized cream-colored sweater. It hides my figure. My hair is swept back into a sloppy ponytail. I cross my legs at the knee and slouch back into my seat.

Miss Black lifts one of her perfectly plucked brows. She's not happy with me.

I protest calmly. "You said make them want more. I don't see a problem here. The only two clients I've been with are asking for me. How's that a bad thing?" I'm trying to keep my voice level. This is about Sean, but she hasn't said that yet.

"Miss Stanz, it's concerning. The nature of your relationship with Mr. Ferro—"

"I don't have a relationship with Mr. Ferro." I can say that because it's true. We're barely friends. Half the time it feels like I'm walking on sand with him. The earth keeps shifting under my feet. I never know which version of Sean I'm with. The dark version scares the crap out of me and I know that's the Sean I'll have if Black puts us together this weekend. I kind of hope she does. I want all this twisted secret stuff he's hiding to be forced out in the open, but then again it might be too much.

She stares at me. "You've done something to both of these men. I have no idea what's between you and Mr. Ferro, but don't you dare tell me that it's nothing. You've been seen together outside of work—"

"By accident. It was a coincidence. What do you want me to do if I bump into Henry Thomas? Blow him off? He might let me, but you already know that Mr. Ferro won't. He's kind of demanding." I make a face and look down at my hands.

"I'm going to say this plainly. If I catch you in a relationship outside of work—if you have any sexual partners at all—I will demand that you return every penny you've earned here. I don't play games Miss Stanz."

"Neither do I." I sit up straight in my seat and lean forward, resting my hands on her dark desk. "Tell me why I haven't been fired? If you think I'm being some sort of deviant—"

She cuts me off. "You are some sort of deviant. You're a call girl. You lie to men for a living and apparently you are very good at it. Of course, I expect you to take your clients in on the side. It cuts out my share and you get paid more for less work. Meanwhile, I'm the one protecting you girls and screening the men. I won't stand for it Avery."

"I am not taking in any business on the side." I look straight into her eyes and try not to laugh. Like I would do such a thing? "I can barely get through a night without throwing up on the guy."

"I'm not naïve. You play the part well, but I know it's an act." I open my mouth to explain but she raises her hand. "Enough. You know the penalty if you get caught. As for this weekend, you'll be double booked since both men are asking for you."

I gape at her. "What?"

Miss Black is no longer looking at me. She's writing something on the legal pad in front of her. "Well, you didn't expect me to turn them away, did you? Mr. Ferro wants you on Friday and Saturday evening. When I told Mr. Thomas that you were booked solid this weekend, he asked if it would be possible to reserve you for Sunday afternoon. We made the schedule work.

"However, I must say, I am leery of Mr. Ferro. Your last meeting alone with him didn't end well, however he was at the meeting with Thomas." She pauses and cocks her head at me, like she just realized something. "You're playing them against each other." Respect flashes in her eyes. "I didn't think you had it in you. You did something—at that dinner—and made them compete for you. I'm impressed." She sweeps her eyes over me like she's seeing me for the first time.

Holy crap is she wrong, but I'm not stupid enough to tell her that. Plus she's not pissed at me for the moment, so I just flash her a cheesy smile. Yup, that's me. Super Slut. Someone should give me a cape. I wonder if I can laugh like an evil villain, but I don't try. Black will think I'm insane. Maybe I am.

Dr. Pratz said to get my hours shaved back and Black is piling them on—and right at the end of the semester. If I work all weekend, I won't have time to finish my papers. I'm caught in the middle and not sure what to do. Since I don't really have a choice, I just nod.

"Miss Stanz," she says as I stand to leave. "Don't you want to know what your take of the fee is this weekend?" *No, not really. Okay, maybe a little.* I nod. She pushes a little white card toward me. It's a lot of money, not as much as I was supposed to get from the first time, but still a lot. "It's impressive."

"It's something."

"You don't sound happy."

I smirk at her. "This is no place for happiness, Miss Black. This is business."

"I'm glad you understand."

CHAPTER 9

It's the end of the week already. I'm sitting across from Marty in the lab. Everyone else has finished, except one girl who was ditched her lab partner. She's pulling double duty. I feel bad for her. If Marty wasn't around, that would be me.

Marty measures something and sets it aside. I write down the number on our worksheet. He glances at me quickly and goes back to work. He's been so tense lately. The other night when he picked me up in

Babylon was weird. It was the only night that I didn't have nightmares. I wonder if it was him—if it was Marty that chased the dreams away. But that's silly. I'm staring at the side of his face.

"What are you thinking about?" he asks.

"The other night, when you picked me up in front my parents' house, I wanted to ask you something. It's bothering me, because I don't really remember. I was kind of out of it."

He nods and looks up at me. Marty is wearing clear goggles. He pulls them off. His gaze lifts and he looks over my shoulder at the girl working alone and then back at me. "What do you want to know?"

I lean in and lower my voice, knowing that it'll sound wrong if I'm overheard. "Did you sleep with me? I mean, you were in the bed with me?" Marty's eyes lock with mine. My stomach dips and goose bumps cover my arms and tickle the back of my neck. I swallow hard, trying to force that feeling back down. Ignoring it, I blink like I inhaled too many lab chemicals and smile at him.

"It's the only night I didn't dream…well, have nightmares. I was wondering why."

Marty nods slowly. "I slept next to you." He turns to the table and puts his goggles back on. He flexes his fingers before grabbing a beaker and pours a clear liquid inside. I jot down how much. He doesn't look at me. "You started whimpering after you fell asleep. When I touched you it stopped."

"So you held me all night?"

He doesn't look at me. "Something like that."

I want him to look at me. Something's going on with him. Friends don't act this way. Mel would have woken me up. Marty's shoulders are so tense. I touch his arm gently. He fumbles the beaker and drops it. The contents spill on the counter as the beaker rolls in a circle. He swears and darts across the room for paper towels. The cabinet where they are supposed to be is empty. "I'll be right back."

I sit back down on my stool and stare at the spill.

The girl behind me clears her throat. I turn and look at her. "He's into you, you know."

I smile at her and shake my head. "Nah, he's into guys."

She smirks and looks down at her worksheet. She measures and writes the answer before saying, "That may be, but he's totally into you, too. He's always looking at you like you're too good to be true. It's the puppy love face. He's got it bad."

She's crazy. I laugh and feel really uncomfortable. "He does not."

"Well, don't say you didn't know when he makes a move on you. If you shoot him down, it'll crush him. And from the looks of it, you guys are friends. He probably doesn't want to screw things up."

I start to say something but Marty walks in with a roll of paper towels. The girl said what I already know, but I still can't believe it. I can't see it. I can't picture Marty pining over me. I can't picture him kissing me or anything else, either. It's too weird.

After he cleans everything up, he says, "So, you working this weekend?"

It seems cruel to tell him. I mean, if he likes me hearing all this has got to be killing him. "Marty?"

He looks up. "Yeah?"

I almost say it. I almost ask, but I can't. I don't want to lose him. I couldn't handle it. I smile and lower my gaze. "Yeah, I'm working, but I wish I wasn't."

Marty gives a weak smile and goes back to work. We finish the assignment in silence. After we put everything away and leave the lab, Marty walks next to me. My heart is beating too fast. My palms are slick and hot. I grip my books tighter and hold them against me. The sky is gray, like it might snow again.

Marty stops. He reaches out and takes my elbow so I turn to him. The sun is weak and the air is cold. It'll be night soon. "I need to tell you something."

If I didn't feel squeamish before, I do now. I don't want him to say it. I have no idea what to do if he does. "Oh?" My mind is reeling, trying to backpedal out of this mess. I glance around frantically, looking for anyone walking by that I might know.

"Yeah, it's important." I glance up at him. Looking into his eyes, I silently plead *Don't do it...Don't, don't, don't*. He breaks my gaze and looks down at the ground between us. "Every time I go to say it, something happens, but I have to tell you. I need for you to know."

No, no, no!

"Avery, I'm not gay."

I expected him to say he had feelings for me, that he's madly in love with me or something like that. I stare at him slack-jawed. "What?"

He won't look at me. "It wasn't supposed to happen this way—"

"What are you talking about?"

His brown eyes flick up and meet mine. "When I first met you, you were kind of intense. Every guy that tried to get near you..." He makes an aggravated sound in the back of his throat and runs his fingers through his hair, tugging hard. "No one could get near you. When you assumed I was gay, I didn't correct you."

I start laughing. "You're really funny. There's no way in hell you would have pretended to be gay to be friends with me."

I punch his arm lightly and smile at him, like this is all a big joke, but Marty doesn't smile back.

"Actually, that's exactly what I did." Marty is looking at his shoe. He flicks his eyes up for half a second and what I see sends a chill down my spine.

I step away from him, shaking my head. "You wouldn't lie to me, not like that—not about that."

Marty steps towards me and hesitates. "I wanted to know you. I heard you talking to Mel and saw you around and—"

"You lied to me?"

"I never said I was gay." The worry in his eyes kills me, but I can't believe he did this. I can't fathom why he kept this charade going for all this time. Everyone thinks he's gay. The depth of the deceit is unfathomable.

"But you lied to me. You let me think it. You didn't say *Hey, I'm straight* and correct me. Damn it, Marty!" Anger bursts through my veins. I pump my fists at my sides, trying to reign in my temper. I don't want to lose him, but this is unacceptable. He's been lying to me. He's seen me and held me in ways he shouldn't have.

"How could you!" I rush at him and slam my palms into his chest. "How could lie to me!"

I do it again. Marty won't look at me, but all the people walking across the quad stop to watch. When I push him a third time, he snaps out of it. Marty grabs my wrists and blocks me. He pushes me away. "I was lonely like you, okay. Maybe you haven't noticed, but you're not the only one alone here, Avery. We got along, you made me laugh, and I thought you liked to have me around. I'm sorry I didn't tell you sooner. Every time I tried, something came up. I didn't mean to mislead you. It was never supposed to get like this."

"Like what? Like one of my best friends stabbed me in the back? Like one of my best friends has been lying to me all this time. Damn it Marty! What am I supposed to do with this?"

"There's something else."

I hold up my index finger and shake it back and forth in front of his face. "Don't say it. Never say it."

He looks down at me. "There's only one way forward. I have to tell you—"

"Don't say it—"

"I love you." I make a crazy sound and spin around and stomp my foot. Marty follows me, explaining, "I'm madly in love with my best friend. I can't help it. I can't stop it. I watch you in silence. I say nothing, but I can't do it anymore. You like these guys who don't give a shit about you. You're making a mistake."

Hysterical laughter bubbles up my throat. "*I'm* making a mistake? Me? Really, that's how you want to play this." I want to say more, but I can't. I can't burn this bridge. Tears sting my eyes. I can't let it go. "What did you think would happen when I found out? Did you think I'd just overlook it? That was one of the biggest secrets you had and you told me. I told you things about me because of that. I let you in because you trusted me with your fake fucking secret."

I press my eyes closed and suck in a slow breath. When I look up, Marty is watching me. He looks terrified, but I can't help him. I can't gloss over it like nothing happened. My fists tighten at my sides. I know how this will end. I'm an idiot. All my friends lied to me. They let me believe whatever I wanted. I didn't know them at all.

I've been quiet too long. The crowd watching us disperses. Marty finally speaks. "Avery, say something."

Grief weighs heavily on me, crushing my shoulders and souring my stomach. "There's nothing to say." I walk away without another word. Marty stands in the quad with his hands at his sides. He doesn't follow. He doesn't beg for my forgiveness.

CHAPTER 10

By the time I'm back at the dorm, I'm fuming. I can't believe Marty lied to me this whole time. I'm not really watching where I'm going smack into someone's shoulder. I glance up and see Mel swallow back down the sharp words that were about to blast into me for bumping her.

"Sorry. I'm kind of—" I don't know what I am. I stop talking and fold my arms over my chest. "Where are you off to?"

"Wrong question. Where am I coming back from? And the answer is Black's. And she told me some twisted shit, so let's chat." Mel jerks her head to the side and I turn back and follow her to her room.

"What twisted stuff was she saying about me?" I ask as I slump into Mel's perfectly pink chair. I steeple my fingers and arch an eyebrow at her.

Mel laughs and sits on the edge of her bed. "She said that you're pulling a double this weekend, as in two guys. Is that true?"

"Well, yeah, but not at the same time." My mind goes back to that list at Miss Black's. I said I'd do anything. I didn't even look to see if a *ménage à trois* was on there. It probably is. My eyes flick up to Mel's.

"Avery, what the hell are you doing?" Mel has her hands in her lap. She leans forward and rests her elbows on her knees. "I heard what you said at Sean's last week. You went bat-shit crazy, by the way."

I laugh at her. "That wasn't bat-shit crazy."

"No. I distinctly remember you saying you didn't want this. You didn't want this life. You were talking about Black. You said you couldn't do it anymore, but here you are signing up to fuck two guys in one weekend. Have you lost your mind?"

"I don't have a choice, do I? Black is pissed at me. She's always pissed at me. If I didn't say I was open to anything, she would have tossed me by now." I can't let that happen. I have to finish what I started. I need to get my degree so I can get on with my life. This is just a stepping-stone; at least, I thought it was.

Mel looks like she doesn't know what to say. She finally says, "You're not cut out for this. You're too soft. When I suggested it, I had no idea. Avery, you should call Black and bow out."

"You think I should quit?"

"I think you should to cut yourself off from Sean, and go after that other guy. Black said he's in love with you. It would fix your money problems and you seem to like the idea of screwing around with one guy. Who knew you were Miss Monogamy?"

I tense. "Henry is not in love with me."

Mel shrugs and sits up. "Say what you want, but you have a problem. And it's the self-destructive exploding kind."

I don't know what to say. I look at the hole in my jeans and pick at the frayed fabric. "You don't think I can do it?"

She shakes her head. "No. I'm sorry I brought you there. The only way you can go through with this is if you change and become so apathetic that you don't care who does you. Do you want to be that girl?"

"Are you that girl?"

Mel flinches like I slapped her. "What the fuck? No, I'm not that girl! I like my job. I have one client on most weekends. One guy. It fits into my idea of normal. This isn't normal for you. In what universe would you sleep with two guys back-to-back like that? In what universe would you do it when you know they hate each other? Even if you were a spiteful bitch, which you're not, you still wouldn't do that. This reality you've made doesn't mesh inside your head. There's only one outcome when things get like that and it ain't pretty."

I swallow hard. My eyes shift back and forth before I look up at her. "Henry doesn't want sex, not yet."

She laughs, like I'm funny. "What? So how far are you going with him this weekend? Does he know you're fucking Sean first?"

I shake my head. "No, I don't think so. Henry wanted to date me. He's pretending that we—"

Mel shakes her head. Her huge earrings swing back and forth. "No. That is not okay. That's when things get messed up. The guy will think he's with you."

"Henry knows he's not."

"But it feels like he is. I'm telling you, this is a bad plan, Avery. Get out of it."

I glance at my hands and turn my palms over. "I never thought I'd do stuff like this, you know? I never thought I'd have to. Pratz wants me to cut back my hours. He said if I don't, grad school isn't a possibility. They'll admit me, but I won't be able to keep up. Then Black hires me out for the entire weekend." Glancing up at Mel, I say, "I thought I'd find someone, you know? I thought he'd save me from all this, but no one came. I'm the only person who can save me and this is the only way to do it."

"You're sacrificing yourself. I'm telling you, once you do this—I mean really do it—you won't be the same. And once you start taking a client every night, there's no going back. The person you were before will be gone, whether you want to lose her or not."

I smile sadly and fold my arms over my chest. "It's strange. Earlier today I argued that people don't change—that they can't. But I know this is changing me, but I can't walk away. There are no other choices, Mel."

"Tell Black no."

"She'll fire me. Gabe said she went to do it and changed her mind. Black's getting an insane amount of money this weekend because of me. I can't walk away…"

"But you want to."

I flick my eyes up and catch her gaze. Hell yeah, I want to. I want to walk away from everything and everyone. There's nothing here for me. My friends lie to me. My lovers are paid. Worst of all, I don't even know who I am anymore. Pressing my lips together, I take a deep breath and nod. "Yeah, I want to, but I must of screwed up my *juju* at some point because the past few years have totally sucked. That explains everything.

I rub my eyes and say, "Guess who's not gay? Guess who's been lying to me since he met me?"

Mel's caramel eyes widen. "Marty's straight? What the hell? He's been lying to you. Oh my God. Oh my God! How could he do that?" She's on the edge of the bed, ready to jump off.

"He said it was the only way to get to know me. He never said he was gay. I assumed he was."

"That little shit. I'm gonna bust his face next time I see him."

"He said he loves me." I stare straight ahead, too overwhelmed to deal with it. He's my friend, but... Damn it. Why did he have to say that?

Mel's mouth forms a little O. She blinks rapidly and whistles. "Holy shit. What'd you do? Did you rip his arms off? Is there a trail of limbs in the quad?"

"No, I'm not you." Mel smirks at me. "I told him off and walked away."

"Marty's your best friend, well, I mean when I'm not around. So what'd he think you would do?"

I shrug. "I have no idea. He said he couldn't take it anymore. When I started working for Black, everything changed. Marty didn't like it."

"Damn, girl." Mel looks pissed. She keeps shaking her head in slow motion with her lips pressed into a thin line. "I'm gonna tear him one."

"Leave it alone. I mean, if you guys are friends, do what you have to, but I don't know what to do with him anymore. It kind of freaked me out." He's so sweet, but I don't think of him like that. That's how we ended up being friends. I'm leery of guys who want to hang around for no reason, because there's never no reason. Even with Marty. Why is every guy I know screwed up?

I look up at Mel. "You really think it'll change me?" I'm talking about working for Black again, about the two men I'm supposed to be with this weekend.

Mel is completely serious. She drops her thick accent and head swaying ways. "It will. And Sean wants some fucked up shit. If that doesn't change you, you're not alive. Throw in the other guy and I don't see how you'll be the same after two nights with crazy and one afternoon with choir boy." Mel looks up at me. "Avery, Sean wants to own you. I've seen guys like that before, but he's ten times more twisted. He'll break you to do it. That's part of what he wants." I'm about to ask how she can be sure when she glances at the floor and pushes off the bed. "I know, because I asked him what he'd do to me."

I swallow hard and pull my feet under my legs. "He told you?"

She nods. "He honed in on the thing that I couldn't—" She makes a noise in the back of her throat and shakes her head. "He found what scares me shitless and he'd use it against me. How can you want to be with someone like that? Does he know what freaks you out like that?"

I nod. "He figured it out already."

"I don't know, Avery. The whole thing is messed up. You're getting into mental fucks and most people don't bounce back from those."

CHAPTER 11

I'm wearing a new silky blue dress with a swishy skirt. Black just sent me off with pride on her face. Sean must have spoken with her at length about me. I pull out the little bracelet and put it on my wrist. This one fits better than the last.

Gabe glances at me in the mirror. It's the third time he's done that.

"Just say it," I finally tell him.

"You're a good kid. Ferro will eat you alive. You shouldn't be with a guy like him."

"What did he do? You act like he's ruthless or something."

Gabe shakes his head. "Black made sure the guys are safe, no convictions, no assault records, but some guys get around that."

I lean forward in the seat. "What are you saying?"

He looks up at me again. I see his old eyes in the mirror. He glances away. "I never said nothing, but Ferro has a temper. The thing with his wife wasn't an accident. He was involved, but the cops never linked it to him. Just because they didn't nail him, didn't mean he didn't do it. But his record's clean so Black okayed him."

What the hell? That can't be right. "Sean was accused of killing his wife?"

Gabe nods. "The bastard was calloused. He didn't even shed a tear. Who does that? I shouldn't say stuff like this, but Miss Stanz, you deserve better than this. Walk away. Tell Black you're through. I'll take you anywhere you want to go, but you should really stay away from that guy. He's not right in the head."

Fuck yeah, Sean's not right in the head. That's glaringly obvious, but from the way he acts, it seems like he misses his wife. I sink back into the seat. I don't blink. I just stare as the city passes by out the window. Gabe blares the horn and curses at another driver as we approach Sean's hotel. Gabe looks back at me, waiting for directions.

I tell him, "Drop me at the curb."

He doesn't say anything else. Gabe slows the car and it comes to a stop. I step out and see Sean Ferro waiting for me. He's wearing a dark suit that makes his eyes look like blue jewels. Stubble lightly dusts his cheeks. Add in the tousled hair and Sean looks like a Greek god.

Gabe's warning flashes through my mind, and mingles with Mel's. Sean's broken, I know that. But I wonder how broken he is. I wonder if he's really responsible for his wife's death. That doesn't make sense. There's no way...

The door of the car is pulled open, but I don't move. A shiver trails down my spine like a premonition of what's to come. "Miss Stanz?" Gabe asks. His voice puts my feet in motion.

I took a chance on Sean. I'm breaking down that goddamn wall that keeps me out. If I get mind fucked while I do it that's one thing, but I can't help but wonder what he's capable of.

CHAPTER 12

"Miss Smith," Sean says and extends me his elbow.

I take it and walk into the building on his arm. "Mr. Jones, how's life treating you?"

"Very well, thank you. I have a beautiful woman on my arm and she's agreed to do very dirty things with me this weekend." Sean grins so hard his dimples show.

My heartbeat quickens. My mind races through what I know about him. I haven't seen a temper, not really. Gabe's warning sticks in my mind. It won't budge. I tense so much that Sean notices. "Don't be nervous Avery. I'll take good care of you."

We step into the elevator and my pulse quickens. I smile nervously. Sean leans into me and presses a soft kiss to my neck. "It took a lot of convincing to get you booked this weekend. Black didn't want me to monopolize her favorite call girl." Sean is leaning into me. His scent fills my head. When we stop, the elevator doors open on the floor with the restaurant. Sean takes my hand and leads me out.

"She didn't let you know?" I glance over at him. "I'm booked on Sunday, too."

Sean stops and looks up at me slowly. The boyish grin vanishes. I wonder if I should have told him. "You're going to Thomas on Sunday?"

I nod slowly, meeting his gaze. "She's happy with my performance." That wasn't the right thing to say. Sean tenses and looks away from me. "Sean, I don't want to lie to you, please don't press it."

"You won't lie to me?" He twists my words slightly, but I nod, because that's what I want. I want more from him. I want the lies and secrets to be gone. I want to know who he is beyond a shadow of a doubt. Sean asks, "Do you like being with him?"

"No. Actually, I wanted to be with you."

"Wanted?" He catches the tense slip. I look away. Sean watches me for a moment. We're standing in front of the restaurant. "So what do you want now?"

Swallowing hard, I say it. "I want to know you. I want to see the real Sean Ferro, demons and all. I want the good, the bad, and the monster within. I want to know you in a way that no one knows you." My eyes wander up his silky smooth tie, over his strong chin, and up his cheeks. I finally look in his eyes. He seems stunned, like I shocked him by saying such a thing.

"No one asks for that."

"I am. I'm asking. Let me in or push me out. I can't do halfway."

Sean nods like he's thinking about it. He takes my hand and we walk to the bar.

Sean orders for us, and then leans on the counter. He avoids my eyes. I wonder what he thinks. I wonder if I found what terrifies him. Two shots of amber liquid are placed in front of us. He gives one to me. "Here's to you, Smitty. You pushed me over the ledge and I'm still falling." He clicks his little glass to mine before downing the shot. Sean places the glass on the counter and orders another. Then he looks over at me and my untouched glass. "You don't drink hard liquor?"

"Not really." More like not ever. I look at it. It's kind of pretty, the way the light shines through the glass.

A crooked smile lines Sean's lips. He lifts the glass and puts it in my hand. "Go on."

I smile at him and lift the glass to my lips. I tip it back, allowing the liquid to slowly flood my mouth. Suddenly it feels like my tongue is on fire. I make a high-pitched whiney sound and swallow it as fast as I can. My tongue juts out of my mouth and I fan it, but it doesn't stop the burning. Sean is watching me with an amused expression on his face. I finally try to scrape the liquor off and drag my tongue across the bottom of my front teeth. Ah! That made it worse. My eyes widen and tear.

Sean can't stop smiling at me. He leans in and puts his hand on my shoulder. "Not really wasn't the right answer, was it?" I shake my head and fan my tongue. I try to talk, but I can't put my tongue back in my mouth without tearing up. Sean bursts out laughing. He pulls me to his chest and kisses my forehead before taking my face between his hands. "You surprise me. No one ever surprises me and somehow you manage. You're adorable. Don't ever change."

CHAPTER 13

After Sean does a few more shots he takes me up to the room. When Sean opens the door, I understand why he stalled at the bar. The room is filled with roses and flickering candles. There's a candelabra on the table, washing the room in golden light. Little tea candles are scattered everywhere. Red rose petals are all over the floor and bed. There's an enormous bouquet of red roses in a vase on the dresser.

I turn and look at Sean, completely surprised. "What is this?"

He smiles softly, suddenly shy. "I thought you'd like it, that's all."

"I'm a call girl. I'll put out without the flowers and candles."

"I'm a romantic—or I used to be—and I wanted to see your face when you walked into the room. I wanted you to know that I'll go through with this, with anything you want. In fact, I'll trade you—anything I want for anything you want." Sean's eyes slip from my face to my dress. It has a low neckline. He presses a kiss to my cheek and lowers his lashes. My heart shudders.

What is he doing? The candles and roses throw me off. People say Sean's cruel. Everyone says that, but I don't see it. I wonder what I'm missing. I wonder if I already see the man they don't realize exists. I glance up at him. "So it's a trade? We'll do exactly what I want for exactly what you want?" He nods. "What does your fetish entail exactly?"

Sean holds my gaze making my stomach flip. He watches me like I'll fade away. He doesn't blink. "Control. I want you, Avery. In every way possible. I want you to quit working for Black. I want you to be with me."

Shock lines my face. "What did you say?"

"I mean it. I want to take care of you. I want you to be with me. I won't share you."

"Then why did you hire me? Why didn't you just ask me this the other day?" I think he's toying with me. I'm lost somewhere between being angry and hopeful.

Sean's lips twitch before smiling softly. "Because you wouldn't have come, you wouldn't have believed me. I'll give you anything I can if you really want to be with me."

"What about Black? I can't quit."

His gaze narrows, becoming more intense. "I can't share you. I won't share you. As it is, I want break Thomas for touching you. I'll pay for whatever you need."

In a million years, I never expected him to say something like that. "Sean, I can't—"

He presses a finger to my lips. "Don't answer now. It's possible that you won't like what you see here this weekend. It's possible you'll never come back, but if you want to stay…" he takes a deep breath and leans in closer to me. Sean's lips are so close to mine. My body tingles, anticipating his touch.

I'm shaken. There are two versions of this man and I can't tell which one is real. Clearing my throat, I stammer, "Who goes first? I mean, do we do things your way or mine?"

"Isn't it obvious?" I shake my head. Sean smiles like he completely adores me. "We'll do things your way first, Avery. Anything you want."

CHAPTER 14

I'm lost in his gaze. I can't stop falling. Everyone thinks he'll destroy me. They think he's going down in flames. I'm not stupid enough to think I can save Sean, but I'm in the same spot in my life. Everything I ever wanted has been blasted to bits. He's the only one who truly understands what it means to be alone and have everything ripped away.

Sean is an island and for some reason he wants me. Time stops and neither of us moves. Sean's breath is warm. It passes over my lips in a gentle breeze. If I lean in and kiss him I'll start something I can't back out of. My heart races faster and faster. There's not enough air, there's never enough around this man. If I step over this line, there's no going back. Nerves shoot through my body and I suck in a shaky breath.

Sean watches me through thick lashes. He presses his forehead to mine. His hand strokes my cheek gently and I lean into his touch. "We don't have to do anything, Avery. We don't—"

I don't let him finish talking. Part of me wants to combust. I want to know, without a doubt, that I'm still alive. I don't want to be numb all the time. I want to feel and touch and be felt. My lips press into his. Sean stops talking and holds my face between his hands. He tilts my head and sweeps his tongue over the seam of my lips. I want to feel everything. I want to feel lust, passion, and fear. I want whatever is on the other side of this.

I hear Mel's voice in the back of my head, *It'll change you.* I hope to God it does. I can't live like this anymore. Most days I feel completely miserable, like I'll never get on with my life.

Sean is kissing me gently as thoughts swirl in my head. They keep coming back to one thing. I can't get through tonight without knowing what tomorrow night holds. Breaking the kiss, I pull away breathless. "I want things your way first."

Sean has that lusty look in his eye. He drinks me in. It makes my stomach twist. "No."

I smile at him and tug on his tie. "Yes." I lean forward and press my lips lightly to his. The touch is so light, so brief that it sends shivers through me.

Sean takes a jagged breath. His eyes are on my lips, wanting more. When he flicks his eyes up, our gazes lock, he says, "No Avery. I want to make sure—"

"So do I. Take me the way you wanted, the way you tried to before."

He's breathing hard, watching me. "I'm not the same man I was before." I don't understand. I shake my head ever so slightly. "I told you there was nothing left to save, that I was screwed up beyond comprehension. I was. There was nothing left worth saving, but then you came along in your crappy car. You fight for every breath you take and you don't back down. I admire that. I admire you, but it's so much more. I was so far gone that I didn't see it, I didn't know I could feel that way again."

My heart starts thumping harder. A shiver climbs up my back and coats my entire body. Is he saying what I think he's saying? "Sean—"

He presses his finger to my lips and silences me. Swallowing hard, he looks up at me. "I regret not saying things in the past. I regret masking my feelings for you. I regret lying to myself, and too many other things to name.

"Avery, I'm so far gone. There's nothing left to love. When you said you loved me, I don't know, it was like I was being attacked. I reacted wrong, but I couldn't stop. No one has loved me, not since Amanda, and not like this." His gaze bores into mine. It's so intense that it makes me squirm. Sean's eyes drift to my lips and back to my eyes. I feel like the world has stopped spinning and I'm floating away. This can't be real.

Sean presses his lips together and smiles at me. "I love you. I love the way you think, the way you blurt out whatever's in your head. I love the way you fly a kite. I love being with you on the beach. I love the way you chased down your car, ready beat the crap out of the guy who stole it. I love that you talk to your parents even though they're gone. I love your fascination with the cold. I love the snowmen. I love that you'll do anything and everything to survive. You're everything wonderful in my life and I don't deserve any of it. I love you, Avery."

Holy shit. Did he say really that? My throat is so tight. It feels like there's an elephant sitting on my windpipe. I can't even choke out a response. I just stand there with my mouth hanging open and my eyebrows creeping up into my hairline.

Sean tangles his fingers in my hair, and looks at me from under his lashes. He leans in close so we're almost lip to lip. He breathes, "You scare the hell out of me."

My voice comes out breathy. "Likewise, Mr. Jones."

He grins. "I don't know what I want anymore, Miss Smith. My life hasn't turned out the way I planned. The only thing I know beyond a shadow of a doubt is that I want you."

Butterflies flutter through my chest. This can't be happening. It can't be. I blink a few times and wonder if I'm dreaming, but my nightmares are never like this. Looking into Sean's face, I need to know. Something happened to his wife and baby. What Gabe said couldn't be true, but I have to know.

My eyes drop to his tie. I stare at it like it's an anchor. I have to ask, but how do I ask him something like that? How can I even mention it now? He said he loves me. I should kiss him and squeal with glee. Instead, these dark thoughts linger and make me question everything.

"Sean…" I whisper his name. Licking my lips, I look up into his face. Every ounce of hope is dashed when he sees my expression. It's like he already knows my question. "Everyone says you're not a person to mess around with, that I should leave you and never look back. They say you're ruthless and coldhearted. I never understood why. I don't see it. Then, I heard something... I have to ask. What happened to Amanda and the baby?"

A current of cold dread runs through my stomach. Sean is so tense. His face loses any trace of the man I was talking to. It becomes a blank slate. Fear flashes in his eyes when looks back at me. "If you're asking that, you already know." He pulls away from me. I watch him walk over to the window and look out at the city. Sean stares vacantly.

I follow him across the room. "What I heard couldn't possibly be true. It doesn't make any sense. I see the way you mourn. You grief is as palpable as mine."

"No, it's not. My grief is nothing like yours." He turns suddenly and our gazes lock. Wild terror burns behind his eyes like he's lost in a horrific memory. Sean steps toward me. "What you heard is true. I killed my wife."

MORE ROMANCE BOOKS BY
H.M. WARD

DAMAGED (A Novel)

DAMAGED 2

STRIPPED

SCANDALOUS

SCANDALOUS 2

SECRETS

THE SECRET LIFE OF TRYSTAN
SCOTT

And more.

To see a full book list, please visit:

www.SexyAwesomeBooks.com/books.htm

CAN'T WAIT FOR H.M WARD'S NEXT STEAMY BOOK?

Let her know by leaving stars and telling her what you liked about THE ARRANGEMENT VOL. 6 in a review!